THE KALEIDOSCOPE

A Kaleidoscope of Multi Genre Tales...

Aryan Majumder

Ukiyoto Publishing

All global publishing rights are held by

Ukiyoto Publishing

Published in 2024

Content Copyright © Aryan Majumder
Illustrated by SRAC

ISBN 9789364946971

All rights reserved.
No part of this publication may be reproduced, transmitted, or stored in a retrieval system, in any form by any means, electronic, mechanical, photocopying, recording or otherwise, without the prior permission of the publisher.

The moral rights of the authors have been asserted.

This is a work of fiction. Names, characters, businesses, places, events, locales, and incidents are either the products of the author's imagination or used in a fictitious manner. Any resemblance to actual persons, living or dead, or actual events is purely coincidental.

This book is sold subject to the condition that it shall not by way of trade or otherwise, be lent, resold, hired out or otherwise circulated, without the publisher's prior consent, in any form of binding or cover other than that in which it is published.

www.ukiyoto.com

This book is dedicated to my paternal grandfather whom I lost recently. He had been an ardent reader of my work and a champion of my successes in life!

CONTENTS

The Betrayal	1
The Full Circle	7
The Dogged Tale	13
The Choice is Yours	21
Cursed	27
The Tinkletown Heroes	33
The Gruesome Graveyard	39

In the dimly lit streets of Tottenham, Greg hastily stuffed a few belongings into a small bag, the urgency fueled by the palpable fear of his stepmother's sinister intentions. The substantial wealth left behind by his late father had transformed into a dangerous beacon, attracting nefarious characters who lurked in the shadows.

The decision to leave his home wasn't easy, but the constant threat of harm compelled him to escape. Paranoia gripped him as he stepped out into the cold night, casting wary glances over his shoulder, half-expecting a hired killer to materialize from the darkness.

A bus to Bristol seemed like a reasonable escape route. The rhythmic hum of the engine and the muted chatter of fellow passengers provided a semblance of normalcy, but Greg's anxiety only intensified. He fidgeted in his seat, nervously scanning the faces around him, convinced that danger loomed with every passing mile.

Seated beside him was a kindly old man, his features softened by age and wisdom. His eyes, however, held a keen awareness that betrayed a life marked by experiences beyond the mundane. Feeling the weight of a sympathetic gaze, Greg couldn't help but let his guard down. The old man spoke with a measured tone, revealing himself to be an ex-military man. Greg, grappling with trust issues, cautiously shared the tale of his treacherous journey.

The old man, named Harold, listened intently, his mind processing the details of Greg's harrowing ordeal. As the bus pressed on, rumbling through the night, Harold contemplated the gravity of the situation. With a nod of understanding, he leaned closer, offering a plan to outsmart the anticipated threat.

"Why head straight to Bristol?" Harold suggested, his voice a low rumble. "We could disembark in Thomson Village, a quiet place off the beaten path. It might throw off anyone following you, buying us time to reassess and strategize."

Desperation painted across his face, Greg hesitated but ultimately nodded in agreement. The decision was made; they would get off the bus in Thomson Village.

The quaint village welcomed them with its stillness as they stepped off the bus. A sense of relief washed over Greg, accompanied by a cautious optimism. Harold, seemingly familiar with the area, guided him through narrow streets until they reached his modest home.

The aroma of brewing tea filled the air as Harold prepared a pot. The cozy interior offered a stark contrast to the fear that had chased Greg from his own home. Seated at the kitchen table, they engaged in conversation, sharing snippets of their lives. For a moment, the weight of impending danger lifted, replaced by a semblance of normalcy.

Greg related the story of his life where after his mother's death his father married a gold digger Matilda. He related how he became conscious of someone hired by her, always following him and overhearing Matilda talk to someone planning his execution.

Harold listened and quite out of context chuckled darkly. "Betrayal is a matter of perspective, Greg. I've seen my fair share of desperate folks trying to escape their fate."

Greg's eyes widened in a mixture of fear and confusion. He set down the cup he was sipping the freshly prepared tea from. Harold leaned against a nearby table, his demeanor casual despite the gravity of the situation. "Let me regale you with stories from my past, Greg. Poisoning, my boy, is an art, a silent killer's craft."

"You see, there are various types of poisoning cases I've encountered," Harold began, pacing around the room. "Some prefer the classics, like arsenic. Tasteless and odorless, it leaves no trace. Others fancy plant toxins – deadly flora from nature's arsenal."

Greg, his strength waning, listened helplessly as Harold continued his macabre monologue.

"I've seen cases where the poison mimics natural illnesses, making it hard to detect until it's too late," Harold mused, his eyes glinting with a sick fascination. "Then there are those who choose unconventional methods, like snake venom or exotic concoctions that defy easy diagnosis."

Greg, now struggling to keep his eyes open, managed to ask, "Why are you telling me this?"

Harold grinned wider. "Knowledge is power, my boy. As you fade away, consider yourself a student in the school of poisons. A lesson paid for dearly."

As Harold continued his morbid tales, Greg's vision blurred further. The room became a disorienting kaleidoscope of shadows, and Harold's voice echoed as if from a great distance.

However, as the minutes ticked by, an uneasiness settled over Greg. He noticed Harold's keen observation, the way his eyes lingered, studying every nuance.

As the conversation flowed, Greg couldn't shake the feeling that something was amiss. Unease settled in Greg's stomach, prompting him to glance around the room for any signs of danger. Harold, seemingly aware of Greg's growing suspicion, maintained his dialogue. He continued to share stories of his military exploits, interspersed with anecdotes from his seemingly ordinary life in Thomson Village. The ticking of a clock on the wall echoed through the room, each second amplifying the tension that hung in the air. Attempting to mask his discomfort, Greg took a last sip of the tea Harold had poured for him. The warmth did little to ease the chill creeping up his spine.

Just as Greg considered excusing himself and tried to get up, Harold leaned in, his voice a low whisper cutting through the silence. "I think, you were right, Greg. You were being followed, but not by who you thought."

"What do you mean?" squeaked Greg.

Greg's heart pounded in his chest as he stared at Harold, disbelief and terror intertwining in his eyes. The room, once a haven, now felt like a trap closing in on him. Paralyzed by shock, Greg attempted to rise from his chair, but his limbs betrayed him. He summoned his last reserves and hauled his body up trying to shove last Harold. After all he was an old man, how can he stop Greg? But he was stopped in his act by Harold's chuckle...he said "my boy, my job is already done. Sad you didn't realize when I spoke of poison that I had doctored your tea. This poison my dear will take your life gently without causing too much pain. Matilda was kind enough not to demand a bloody execution. You are dying Greg...those sensations you are having are due to the lethal poison I infused. It's easier this way you see, I can dig the ground and put your body underneath and no one would know where you vanished! My pockets will be full in no time son. The killer you feared," Harold continued, relishing the moment, "is none other than me."

the full circle

Chapter 1: Echoes of the Past

Arjun Sharma, born in Mumbai and a photographer by profession, had always been drawn to the village of Lyallpur. Whenever he visited Pakistan where his firm had business exposure, he would visit Lyallpur. An inexplicable sense of familiarity washed over him, as if he had walked those narrow lanes and breathed that fresh air in a previous life. The village was famous as the birthplace of the martyr Bhagat Singh. One day during a planned photoshoot In Lyallpur, as Arjun strolled through the village with his friends, a sudden flash of scenes started unfolding before his eyes. He was about to fall off guard by the vivid flashes of images playing in front of his eyes like flashback of a movie. It was as if a forgotten door had creaked open, revealing a hidden chamber within his mind. Images from a time long gone came flooding back. He saw himself as a young boy, running barefoot through the fields, his laughter echoing through the trees. He saw himself sitting by the village well, listening intently to the stories of the elders. These memories were so vivid, so real, that Arjun felt as though he were reliving them. He could almost hear his own voice, the laughter of his friends, the gentle murmur of the wind through the leaves. As the scenes before his eyes continued to unfold, Arjun wondered if he had been a freedom fighter in his past life like Bhagat Singh.

The kaleidoscope of scenes suggested that he had fought valiantly against the British Raj, his heart filled with a burning desire for his country's independence. But his life had been cut short, his dreams shattered by a cruel twist of fate. He had died a martyr, his name forever etched in the annals of history. Arjun stood transfixed beneath a Banyan Tree, wondering if he had been reborn, given a second chance to live the life he had been denied. But if so, fate had played a strange trick on him. He had forgotten his past, his identity. As the echoes of the past reverberated through his mind, Arjun felt a mix of emotions. There was a sense of wonder, a thrill of discovery. But there was also a sense of loss, a longing for the life he had once lived. Was he an accomplice of the great Bhagat Singh? So, Arjun began a journey to unravel the enigma of his past. He delved into the history of Lyallpur, searching for clues that would help him piece together the fragments of his forgotten life.

Chapter 2: The Village of Deja Vu

Arjun's mind raced as he tried to make sense of the vivid memories that had flooded his consciousness. The village of Lyallpur, with its cobblestone streets and ancient temples, felt both familiar and foreign. He explored the village with a newfound intensity, searching for clues that could unlock the secrets of his past. He visited the village elder, an elderly woman who had lived in Lyallpur for generations. She listened intently to Arjun's story, her eyes twinkling with a mixture of curiosity and recognition. "My child," she said softly, "I have heard tales of a brave revolutionary hero who once resided in these very lands. His name was Bhagat Singh, and he fought valiantly against the British." Arjun's heart skipped a beat. Could he be the reincarnation of this legendary figure? The elder's words resonated with the fragments of memory that had haunted him.

As he delved deeper into the history of Lyallpur, Arjun discovered that Bhagat Singh had been a beloved son of the village. He had led a life of courage and sacrifice, inspiring his fellow villagers to fight for their freedom. But fate had a cruel twist in store. Bhagat Singh wanted to avenge the death of Lala Lajpat Rai ji but instead was prosecuted for killing of a junior British police officer due to mistaken identity. The villagers had mourned his loss deeply, but they had never forgotten his legacy. Arjun felt a profound connection to this tragic story. The more he learned about Bhagat Singh, the more he recognized himself in the hero's spirit. The village of Lyallpur, once a stranger, now felt like a home he had long been searching for.

Chapter 3: Unravelling the Enigma

Arjun delved deeper into the enigma of his past; he encountered a series of tantalizing clues. The villagers, intrigued by his uncanny familiarity with their history, began to share their own stories and legends. One elderly woman, known as Amma, recounted a tale of a valiant Bhagat who had been imprisoned during the British Raj. Bhagat Singh had fled Lahore after the killing of the British officer and taken refuge in Kolkata, where he had lived in hiding until he again resurfaced to and lobbed a bomb at Central Legislative Assembly in Delhi. He had surrendered then. Arjun sought out the old jail records and discovered a striking resemblance between his own facial features and a faded photograph of a shaved Bhagat Singh. The similarities were uncanny, down to the distinctive scar on his left cheek. As Arjun pieced together the fragments of information, a startling realization dawned upon him. Could it be possible that he was the reincarnation of Bhagat Singh, himself? The thought filled him with a mix of awe and trepidation.

He confided in his friends, who were initially skeptical but gradually came to believe his extraordinary tale. Together, they embarked on a quest to uncover the truth behind Arjun's past life. They revisited history and read through the details that described Bhagat Singh's unwavering patriotism, his selfless sacrifice, and his tragic end. As Arjun read, he felt an overwhelming surge of emotion. The words seemed to resonate deep within his soul, as if they were confirming his long-held suspicions. With each new revelation, the enigma of Arjun's past slowly began to unravel. The fragments of memory, the uncanny similarities, and the historical evidence all pointed to an extraordinary truth: Arjun felt that he was indeed the reborn spirit of the village's legendary freedom fighter, Bhagat Singh.

Chapter 4: Memories Resurface

Days turned into weeks, Arjun's strange visions and feelings only intensified. He refused to go back to the city. The more time he spent in Lyallpur, the more vivid his memories became. He began to recall specific events, faces, and conversations that seemed to belong to a life he had lived long ago. One afternoon, as he sat by the village well, a familiar voice caught his ear. It was the sound of a young woman singing a traditional folk song. As the melody washed over him, a wave of nostalgia swept through Arjun. He felt as though he knew the song by heart, as if he had sung it countless times before. Curiosity consumed him, and he followed the sound until he came to a small cottage. Outside, a young woman was sitting on a charpoy, her hands deftly plucking at an ektara. Her voice was sweet and clear, carrying the same haunting melody that had triggered his memories. As Arjun approached her, the woman looked up, her eyes widening in surprise. "Do I know you?" she asked, her voice trembling slightly. Arjun stared at her, his heart pounding in his chest. Her features were unfamiliar, yet something about her seemed so deeply ingrained in his memory. "I don't think so," he replied, his voice barely a whisper. "But I feel like I should. "The woman smiled, a hint of recognition in her eyes. "My name is Durga," she said. "My family has lived in this village for generations." Arjun's mind raced as he tried to make sense of the situation. Could it be possible that he had known Durga in his past life? The thought filled him with a strange mix of excitement and trepidation. Could this lady be Durgawati Devi who had impersonated as Bhagat Singh's wife and helped him take refuge after the Officer Saunder's Murder? The valiant lady had been a freedom fighter herself. Could this young woman be the same lady reincarnated like him. The memories that had been haunting him were not merely fragments of a forgotten past but a connection to a life he had lived before. However, once his reverie broke, he saw there was no one in front of him and he was standing alone as if the conversation with the young woman was just a figment of his imagination. He was immediately assailed by images of a young man lobbing bomb in the assembly and felt shivers down his spine, as if he was watching himself in action!

Chapter 5: The True Identity Revealed

Arjun forced his mind to piece together the fragments of his past life. The images that had flashed through his mind were not mere hallucinations; they were echoes of a time when he had been indeed the legendary Bhagat Singh, fighting for the independence of his beloved country. He had witnessed countless horrors during the struggle, but his spirit remained unbroken. However, fate had a cruel twist in store for him. After surrendering to the British he was tried in court and was hanged till death by the British Raj for the murder of officer P. Sauders. As his life ebbed away, he had uttered a heartfelt wish: to be reborn in free India and continue the fight for justice. Unbeknownst to Arjun, his wish had been granted. He had been reincarnated as an ordinary man in the present day, but the memories of his past life were dormant within him. As the truth dawned upon Arjun, he felt a profound sense of awe and destiny. He realized that his inexplicable connection to Lyallpur in Pakistan was not a coincidence; it was the village where Bhagat Singh had spent his childhood. The people he had met and the experiences he had shared there were all echoes of his former life. With his identity revealed, Arjun embarked on a new mission. He dedicated himself to honoring the legacy of Bhagat Singh and continuing the fight for a just and equitable society. He used his newfound knowledge and insights to inspire others and to remind them of the sacrifices made by those who had paved the way for their freedom. And so, Arjun Sharma, with the indomitable spirit of the Indian freedom fighters who had fought for a better tomorrow, decided to work for rural development. He decided to join an NGO and try to help the poor, destitute and the marginal populations to have a better life through self-help and cooperative approaches, just as Bhagat Singh would have wanted, had he lived to see India Independent in 1947. Life had come to a full circle for a valiant son of the soil.

In the bustling city of Pawington, animals ruled the streets while humans served as their loyal pets. It was a world turned upside down, where dogs, cats, and even birds held positions of power and authority. Among them was Fido, a clever cocker spaniel with a knack for solving mysteries around town.

Fido was known far and wide for his sharp wit and keen sense of smell. He had a reputation for being able to sniff out trouble before anyone else even knew it existed. His owner, Mrs. Whiskers, was a wealthy Siamese cat who had taken a liking to the plucky little spaniel and had appointed him as her personal detective.

One day, as Fido was lounging in the sun outside Mrs. Whiskers' luxurious mansion, a frantic squirrel came running up to him, chittering in distress. "Fido, Fido, you have to help us! Someone has stolen all the acorns from the park!"

Fido's ears perked up at the news. He knew that the park was a favorite gathering spot for the city's animals, and the theft of the acorns was sure to cause chaos. Without hesitation, he sprang into action, his nose twitching as he followed the scent of the stolen nuts.

As he made his way through the city, Fido questioned the other animals he passed, gathering clues and piecing together the puzzle. He soon discovered that a mischievous raccoon named Bandit was behind the theft. Bandit had been hoarding the acorns in his den, planning to sell them for a hefty profit.

Fido wasted no time in tracking down Bandit's hideout, where he found the raccoon surrounded by piles of stolen acorns. With a bark and a growl, Fido confronted Bandit, demanding that he return the nuts to their rightful owners.

Bandit tried to put up a fight, but Fido was too quick and too clever for him. With a few well-placed barks and a bit of intimidation, he managed to convince Bandit to give up the stolen acorns and promise never to steal again. The animals of Pawington rejoiced at Fido's success, throwing a grand celebration in his honor. Mrs. Whiskers was especially proud of her clever detective, showering him with treats and praise.

But Fido knew that his work was never done. As long as there were mysteries to solve and injustices to right, he would be there, ready to sniff out the truth and bring justice to the city of Pawington. And so, the clever cocker spaniel continued his adventures, solving mysteries and keeping the peace in a world where animals ruled and humans were their loyal pets.

Few days later...

In the town of Petropolis, the towering buildings are occupied by a diverse community of animals, each with their own role to play. The streets bustle with activity as cats scurry on their missions, birds fly overhead, and dogs like Fido can be seen walking their human 'pets.' Fido, a large and loyal canine, watches over his human companions with a sense of duty and protectiveness, his keen eyes missing nothing as he stands tall as the self-appointed protector of the town. Despite his vigilant watch, Fido is haunted by a recent spate of kidnappings that have left the town in fear, especially after a beloved puppy from a neighbouring family went missing under mysterious circumstances, driving the town's anxiety to new heights.

The tense air in Petropolis reaches a breaking point when news spreads like wildfire that the reckless Thunder mouses have kidnapped a litter of innocent puppies. The sheriff, a gruff and no-nonsense bulldog, is at a loss, declaring the case unsolvable. But Fido's heart aches at the cries of the puppy's desperate mother, and with a determined gleam in his eye, he makes the decision to take matters into his own paws. The time has come for Fido to step out from the shadows and into the spotlight, ready to prove himself and save the day, embarking on a treacherous journey to track down the vile culprit.

Just when Fido is beginning to feel a flicker of hope after uncovering a potential lead that points toward the Thunder mouses, a shocking revelation shatters his confidence. The thugs of the town, led by a cunning snake in a suit, are now hot on his trail, aiming to silence him and bury the truth. Fido's moment of supposed victory at identifying the kidnappers has turned into a dangerous game of cat and mouse, putting not just the missing puppies in peril, but also his own life.

As Fido delves deeper into the mystery, it becomes painfully clear that the city he thought he knew is concealing dark and sinister forces. With each step he takes, the noose tightens around his neck, leaving him with fewer allies to trust and nowhere to turn for help. The enemy's grip on Powerout Alley, the shadowy heart of the criminal underbelly, tightens, leaving Fido isolated and vulnerable, facing threats from all sides.

In a heart-wrenching betrayal, Fido's closest friend, a cunning fox Named Sly, succumbs to the seduction of power and switches sides, leading the kidnappers straight to the doorstep of the exhausted Fido, ready to end his noble quest once and for all. With the clock ticking and darkness looming, Fido is left with nothing but his wits and unwavering determination as he stands on the edge of true defeat, the weight of his failures pressing down on his shoulders like a heavy shroud of despair.

In his darkest hour, Fido is granted a serendipitous encounter with a wise old owl, an oracle of truth who imparts to him the invaluable lesson that courage and compassion are the engines that fuel the heart of a hero. Gaining a newfound sense of purpose and a deep well of inner strength, Fido rises from the ashes of his despair, his spirit unbroken and his resolve unshakable. With his loyal companions, the resourceful squirrels and the stealthy raccoons, by his side, Fido hatches a daring plan to take down the kidnappers and liberate the trembling puppies from their clutches.

Finale

The decisive showdown between good and evil unfolds in the heart of Powerout Alley, as Fido, fueled by his righteous fury and resolute courage, faces off against the tyrannical snake and his minions in a battle of wills. With clever strategies, the help of newfound allies, and a touch of heartwarming ingenuity, Fido outsmarts the villains and emerges victorious, emerging as a hero in the eyes of the town, both animal and human alike. As the sun sets on the horizon, painting the sky with hues of triumph and hope, Fido's bark rings out in a triumphant chorus, with the streets of Petropolis alive with cheers and praises for their indomitable protector. The bond between animals and their human 'pets' grows stronger, and Fido, standing tall and proud, knows that his courage and unwavering determination have saved not just the puppies, but the very spirit of the town itself.
Few months passed and then...

Fido the cocker spaniel had always been a curious and adventurous dog. He loved exploring the city where animals ruled, where cats lounged in cafes and birds flew freely in the sky. But one day, Fido stumbled upon a mystery that would change his life forever.

As he was walking through the bustling streets, Fido noticed a group of squirrels whispering to each other in a dark alley. Intrigued, he decided to follow them. The squirrels led him to a hidden underground tunnel, where he saw a group of rats huddled together, looking nervous.

"What's going on here?" Fido barked, his tail wagging with excitement.

The rats looked at each other, unsure of what to say. Finally, one of them spoke up. "We're in trouble, Fido. The cats have been disappearing one by one, and we fear we might be next."

Fido's heart raced with fear. He knew he had to do something to help his fellow animals. "I'll get to the bottom of this," he declared, determination shining in his eyes.

With the help of his friends, a wise old owl and a mischievous raccoon, Fido set out to uncover the truth behind the mysterious disappearances. They followed clues and interrogated suspects, all while dodging danger at every turn.

As they delved deeper into the mystery, Fido realized that the culprit was none other than a cunning fox who had been kidnapping the cats to sell them to a wealthy collector. With a plan in place, Fido and his friends set a trap for the fox, leading to a thrilling chase through the city streets.

In the end, Fido and his friends managed to capture the fox and rescue the missing cats. The city erupted in cheers as Fido was hailed as a hero, his bravery and quick thinking saving the day.
As he basked in the adoration of his fellow animals, Fido knew that he was destined for more adventures in the city where animals ruled. And he couldn't wait to see what mysteries awaited him next.

A year went by when again Pawington and Petrapole were shaken by a crime...

Fido, as always, was known throughout the animal kingdom for his sharp wit and keen sense of smell. He was always ready to help his fellow creatures in need. One day, a terrible crime shook the animal world. The beloved lion king, Leo, was found dead in his den. The animals were in a state of shock and confusion. Who could have committed such a heinous act?

Fido knew he had to do something to solve the mystery and bring the culprit to justice. He set out on a quest to uncover the truth, using his keen sense of smell to sniff out clues and his quick thinking to piece together the puzzle.

As Fido delved deeper into the investigation, he discovered that there were many animals with motives to harm the lion king. From jealous hyenas to power-hungry elephants, the suspects were numerous and the trail was cold.

But Fido was determined to crack the case. With the help of his friends, a wise old owl and a mischievous monkey, he followed the clues to the heart of the mystery. And in a thrilling climax, Fido finally revealed the true culprit behind Leo's murder.

The animal world was astounded by Fido's bravery and intelligence. He became a sensation, hailed as a hero by all the creatures of the kingdom. Fido's name was known far and wide, and he was celebrated as the greatest detective in the animal world.

And so, Fido the cocker spaniel had solved the murder mystery that had baffled the animal kingdom. With his quick wit and sharp senses, he had proven that even the smallest of creatures could make a big difference in the world. And his story would be told for generations to come, inspiring animals everywhere to follow in his paw prints.

The great strategist Acharya Chanakya said, "There is some self-interest behind every friendship. There is no friendship without self-interests. This is a bitter truth."

"Acharya, does that mean there is nothing called true friendship?" asked King Chandragupta. "My Lord, you must choose your friends wisely, and never reveal you plans to anyone in whatever form or feature. Friendship is a glorious name given to congenial relationship to fructify one's self interest."

It was my first day at the University of Hertfordshire in Hatfield. Being an Indian, in the middle of all these UK people...It was tough. I moved to Hatfield when I was 14 from Calcutta...my father got a transfer. Growing up like this in the middle of the UK...that too in my teen years was a little difficult. I always had different interests than the North English kids present here. I was never interested in rugby or football...I found it too physical. I never enjoyed partying like them...instead I would prefer reading a book. I was completely different from them ... which is the sole reason why I had no friends. But yeah... coming back to the topic...today was the first day of the year. I wasn't too excited to be honest. As usual I would have no friend! And I would completely have to slog through the year. That's when I saw Sameer for the first time. He was a tall, tanned and curly haired boy with spectacles. He was sitting in the corner of the class, probably was too shy to talk and had no friends. The thing that struck me the most was that he was not an original resident of the UK. So, I decided to go and talk with him.

"Hey" I said, approaching him. Sameer looked up at me blankly.

"My name is Karan" I said.

"Cool name" he replied. He probably couldn't make out that I wanted to start a conversation with him.

"What's your name?" I asked.

"Sameer" he replied a little awkwardly. Seeing his awkwardness, I understood his problem. "Can I sit beside you?" I asked. After he affirmed, I asked him "Listen man... we both seem to have the same problem, that is making friends! So, let's help each other out." Sameer smirked. "Well then, why are you being so formal?" "I've never had friends before...so bear with me" I said. "There's a first time for everything I guess?". From there onwards we started talking. We talked until all our classes ended. Boys become friends so soon. I got to know that Sameer originally lived in Watford, but had to shift here due to some reasons. He was a little weak in studies. But he still managed somehow.

We both had the same orthodox brown parents,so had the same problems. I was proud of myself thinking that I finally made a friend. And coincidentally, he lived just three blocks away from me! That was surely an advantage for me. However, once I couldn't go to school for 2 to 3 days, because I was sick. The next day when I went, I saw Sameer had made some new friends! When I entered the hallway, he saw me and asked me about my health. "I'm fine don't worry" I said. "Anyways bro...come and meet my new friends" Sameer replied. I followed him to the lockers. There I saw Bryan, Coby and Ash. All of them where the most popular kids of the school. I never spoke to them. "This is my best friend Karan," Sameer said. Somehow, that line gave me confidence. I was never called even a friend by anyone and on hearing this I took a leap of confidence. Bryan replied "I haven't seen your so-called best friend play any sports". I took charge by saying "well I play cricket but there is no school team for that sport."Cricket? That's for boomers," said Coby. The bell rang and we all went to our classes.

I was thinking all day about that "boomer" catchphrase. Did this mean I was not a friend that Sameer deserved? Sameer read my face somehow and said "Don't worry Karan, you are my best friend...I don't care what anyone else says" Hearing this I was happy. I finally got a friend I deserved.

Now, it was time to update myself. I started wearing cool jackets and sweaters instead of t-shirts. I changed my style completely. I threw away my nerdy glasses and got a new frame. I started to explore new hairstyles...and most importantly I started talking with people.

I completely moved out of my old zone. After a few days I saw Bryan and his group again. Quote me when I say this...but they were more popular than Michael Jackson himself in the school. Right now, I have upgraded myself and I just needed friends. So, I asked Sameer to introduce me to them so that I could also talk to them. Sameer agreed and he introduced me to their group.

By this time, Sameer had really become very close friends with Bryan and his friends. Don't get me wrong, but I was a little jealous. My best friend was friends with the most popular guys in the school and I was here just doing nothing.
That struck me hard. And then...I did something. Something malicious. The cunning of the cunning peeps would possibly do this...and me!

After I got introduced to Bryan, aka the popular guy I had started hanging out a lot with him. I stopped hanging out with Sameer and I always gave him excuses. I also joined the popular school group everyone talked about.

Then came January, when the college hosted a fest. Obviously, this year too they hosted one. Everyone was excited. As usual Bryan and his friends were about to pull off some notorious act. When I asked him about it, he said "oh I already told Sameer about the plan. Ask him to inform you as well". Here too, I was a little jealous. Sameer was more of a friend to them then I was. But I heard the plan anyways. They were about to change the calm music of the fest to a lewd one and were about to mess with the disco lights during our college performance. Everything was set up.

But Sameer seemed against the plan. "Destroying the college's reputation for such a silly act in front of thousands of people isn't funny...At least I don't find it so". I was surprised to hear this. This was coming from Sameer, a guy who, like me, never seemed to have the guts to go against the strong ones.

The day of the fest arrived. Bryan and his friends pulled off both their acts perfectly. Our college got humiliated and decided to refrain from hosting any fests for the next 2 years. Everyone in the group was smirking, that was, except Sameer. Next something shocking happened. An anonymous person on Gmail mailed the college administration team a video. A video that showed Bryan, Coby and others changing the music and fooling with the light system. All of them were immediately caught and suspended for 2 weeks. "Once I find which lunatic did this... I'll skin him alive," said Bryan.

That day I was feeling lonely while doing classes and thought of Sameer. I hand ghosted him after meeting Bryan, so had I used him to my own benefit? I kept thinking this the whole day. He was not attending classes, but in the evening, Sameer texted me. He wrote "You won't believe what I did"! He sent me screenshots of him mailing the college office the same video which convicted Bryan and team. SO IT WAS HIM? HE TOOK THE VIDEOS?

I had 2 options, either to keep quiet and appreciate my best friends or to snitch on him. One thing was clear, If I sent these screenshots to Bryan, he would not only cut Sameer off, he would also befriend me as I helped him, and I would become one of the cool kids. I would get the attention of so many people! But...would I be selfish in doing that? Was I thinking too much? I had second thoughts? I was confused. I didn't know what to do. I surely couldn't snitch on my first and only best friend, right? He had introduced me to people. He made me change. I surely can't put him into trouble.

I finally made my decision. Soon I became an anchor friend in Bryan's friend group. I became popular. Very popular. Bryan beat up Sameer very badly. Sameer called and texted me multiple times... I blocked him. He came to my house, but I shooed him away. His reputation at school was ruined. On the other hand...my reputation was like that of Monarch. Well, I'm still guilty of my decision...of what I did. But that's a secret, only I know that. So, I am a good person in front of people, right?

The question of the century should be... Do spirits exist? No obviously. But is there negative energy in and around us? This isn't explainable. But something that happened with me in that mess in North India...will always be an enigma to me, as I remember each and every detail by heart.

I was in Haryana, erstwhile Kurukshetra for my second year in college.

I had just returned from my holidays. But my friend Shiv had not returned yet. So, I was lonely for the first few days. One random Sunday, Krish rang me up. He wanted to spend the day in my room chilling. And I agreed. Krish was a friend of Shiv and we three had become very good friends. Krish lived in a different hostel. So, we couldn't always be together. We planned on watching a movie that day and then order some food later on.

Krish came in later than his promised time and he ordered all the food himself. I was surprised how he all of a sudden had so much money. On asking him he exclaimed "Oh boy, this guy has to be a detective everywhere! I'll tell you about this later on." I didn't want to ask more. Oh! and this reference of being a detective was because I am actually interested in being a detective. But not for humans.

Negative energy has been my point of fascination since I was a kid. I was always interested to know about this paranormal stuff. And I tried a lot of things to encounter the so-called "spirits' ' at 3am... but the only thing I encountered were insects every time. Till now I had never succeeded in experience such a thing. But I never lost hope.
Me and Krish were having dinner. As usual we ran out of topics to talk about. The movie was over. "Oyeh" said Krish "let's go outside and eat below that tree. It would be a great feeling". He pointed at the tree which was outside our whole mess looming ominous on the ground.

Now let me tell you something. The people living here were never allowed to go outside after 7pm, and the landlord would get really angry if we did so. But we broke the rule this time because we didn't care much. Little did I know that this would cause a random turn of events that would affect the next 2-3 years of my life.

Me and Krish sat below the Peepal tree. Eating our thali. Krish suddenly said "Yo Krish...you think this tree is haunted by the spirits?"

Krish would always mock me for my obsession with spirits. So, I played along. "Well maybe ... there is something... or someone present here... You dare not mock them."

Krish led out a roar of laughter. "If you say so Mr Ghostbuste ...Tthen I'll definitely obey you". He went near the tree and looked up and then said "hey you... Or whoever is present...I challenge you to come and punish me for my sins! Ohhh my God will you come draped in a white sheet? Oh my God, will you cry out like in the movie "Conjuring?" Krish threw his leftover plate at the foot of the tree and said "come punish me coward hoooo."

I didn't like this action of Krish. "Stop with your tomfoolery Krish-". Before I could complete the sentence, our landlord came out and shouted "Didn't I tell you to not come out after 7 pm? Go to your rooms both of you" he said. Krish left on his bike and I also went to my room, disturbed and sleepy.

The next day went fast. At night around 11pm, I was watching a movie, when suddenly I heard a knock on the door. I thought to myself "oh, Shiv has finally returned." I went to open the door but then I suddenly remembered that Shiv had messaged me in the evening that he would be returning 2 days later. And no one in the locality knew me. So, who was this?

I looked through the keyhole and I saw no one. I went back to watching my movie and then I heard a knock again. I ignored it thinking someone was pranking. But I heard the knock again. Irritated...I called prantik who lived in the same mess. His room was perpendicular to ours and from his room you could see the doorstep of my room. I called him over the phone and said "hey, can you please check if there is someone at my doorstep?" He did as directed and said, "No, I don't see anyone here". At this point I remembered about the 3 knocks of death. I was scared and I went to sleep grasping the locket my mother gave me. It had God Krishna's picture in it and fell asleep.

The next day I woke up to Shiv's voice who was literally banging on the door. "Did you die or something? Open the door you imbecile!" I opened the door and saw Shiv. "Were you sleeping with your ears plugged?" said Shiv laughing. "Why did you return early?" I asked him. "Oh, I left some of my things here. I'll take it back and will return after a couple of weeks". Shiv was departing that night. So, we planned to spend the day together. We called Krish but he didn't pick up. While we were at brunch, I told him about the Peepal tree incident. But Shiv suddenly got serious. "Look imbecile, I know you are dumb but don't be this dumb, you should follow the landlords orders". "Hey Shiv, why are you so serious?" I asked, surprised. I had never seen him this angry before. Shiv said "look I can't explain anything right now...but I know more people in this mess than you do. Just ... Be safe."

That evening, I returned to our room alone and I had all these thoughts running in my mind but I still tried to fall asleep.

The next day I woke up to Shiv's voice who was literally banging on the door. "Did you die or something? Open the door you imbecile!"

I opened the door and saw Shiv. "Were you sleeping with your ears plugged?" said Shiv laughing.

"Why did you return early?" I asked him. "Oh, I left some of my things here. I'll take it back and will return after a couple of weeks". Shiv was departing that night. So, we planned to spend the day together. We called Krish but he didn't pick up. While we were at brunch, I told him about the Peepal tree incident. But Shiv suddenly got serious. "Look imbecile, I know you are dumb but don't be this dumb, you should follow the landlords orders". "Hey Shiv, why are you so serious?" I asked, surprised. I had never seen him this angry before. Shiv said "look I can't explain anything right now...but I know more people in this mess than you do. Just ... Be safe."

That evening, I returned to our room alone and I had all these thoughts running in my mind but I still tried to fall asleep.

I got woken up by a knock at 2 am. "Rahul... Rahul, please open the door." said Shiv. "Coming" I answered. I washed my face and went near the door to open it. But then...I suddenly remembered something. His train had already left. He had boarded it in front of me. He couldn't come back so fast and even if he did, he wouldn't call me by my first name. He calls me "imbecile". I froze at the spot as the knocks got heavier. I went back to my bed...and pulled the blanket over my head. I grabbed my Krishna locket in my hand. I sat upright in the bed with my head covered and started reciting prayers. And then suddenly I heard a different knock on my bedroom door. It was heavy and a voice which didn't sound anything less than a belligerent one said "open the door."

I suddenly felt my body going out of my control. My legs moved and I stood up like a robot and opened the door.
I still cannot forget what I saw. I saw someone, who was clearly neither Ghost nor Human, a glowering presence from some other era..

"You shouldn't have challenged the powers of the Peepal tree my child. Your friend shouldn't have. He will pay for his sins. And you my child, your obsession and excitement about these will fade away. You will always remember this night but would never be able to narrate it. Now, I know what you are thinking! Who am I? I am the immortal...the cursed warrior...you've heard about me in the stories, I am my child... Ashwathama."

The next morning Krish was found dead in his room. During the investigation it came to light that he was a crypto scammer. His misdeeds were leaked by an anonymous person. No wonder he had suddenly become rich. I was admitted to the hospital after that night and the cause was unknown, however I knew why I fell ill but also realized I would never be able to narrate it to anyone ever, no one would believe me.

To this day, I still remember Him. His presence, His face, the open wound on his forehead where obviously he wore the famous jewel he was born with, and his powers. I remember Him the great Ashwatthama who roamed the earth and punished the errants and lived on forever as the Cursed Immortal.

That summer when I visited Cousin Harold in the village of Tinklerown, I found the locality grim and quiet. Recently a rich old man by tje name of Peter Weise had disappeared! No one knew where he went. The last anyone saw of him was his orphan nephew who had taken a Polaroid snap of his Uncle, with his new camera. The servants also did not know anything. He had gone out for a walk like always and never came back! The nephew reported the incident to the police and was completely crestfallen. Harold had an uncle in the police department, and he had managed to get some inside information that police had looked for him everywhere, in fact they had also visited the William Mansion which was known to be a haunted house since William Chardoney, the owner had committed suicide there. The House was old and constructed in 1800s.They had found his briefcase there which he was carrying when he went for a walk that day, but there was no trace of him.

Four of us, consisting of myself, Harold, Lewis, and Ben finally gathered up the courage to visit the house for our own bit of investigation. We still couldn't believe how in 24 hours or less we came up with a plan to explore a HAUNTED HOUSE, that too in this very village.

The front door was wide open as usual. It was the same, when the police had visited. There seemed as if it had no connection with the outer world, as if the whole house was still in the 1800s. There were no animals around the whole area, not even a single bird. All of us were a little agitated, when suddenly Ben broke the silence.

"Oh, c'mon there is nothing in there. This is all just a piece of crap. Most probably... Mr Wiese has been abducted by others...And it has got nothing to do with the house." Lewis seemed a little irritated with this.

"Oh, Ben stop with your folkloric and baseless conclusions. The police found Mr Wiese's briefcase inside the house.... We all know it's related to this place.

"And Mr. Smarty Pants" said Ben "how do you know the briefcase wasn't planted?" At the mention of this, I remembered something! "The briefcase wasn't planted, Ben," I replied. I quickly opened the image of the newspaper on my phone. "Look ... in this picture the briefcase has a white-coloured tag on its handle, and it's the same tag that Mr. Wiese had on his briefcase when he was last seen in the picture taken by his nephew. Both the tags have a picture attached to it. Probably the Polaroid he had taken, was with his wife ... Perhaps their last photo with each other." My deduction seemed to impress all of the three musketeers.

"Brilliant deduction. Seems like the tikka masala has been working... Hasn't it Aj?" Ben questioned jokingly.

After this quick conversation... We entered the House. Harold was quite all along... Because he was frightened of ghosts. But that didn't stop him from using his intelligence. As soon as we entered the house, we saw it was covered in cobwebs and dust. "Blimey ... this house must have been abandoned since the last two hundred years!" Exclaimed Ben. Lewis started to examine each and every corner. I searched the dining room.... While Ben and Lewis searched the two bedrooms. Harold seemed calm and didn't move from the main hall. While in a bedroom, Ben found a big shelf full of alcoholic spirits. "Someone must've drunk their livers out" Ben said. We met again in the main hall ...And as expected, we found nothing. We were discussing when Harold said "see guys... You try to find big details and you miss out the small ones." "And what do you mean?" I asked.

. He touched a Cobweb. "This is fake... this Cobweb is totally fake and sprayed on by foam ... So that it gives the illusion which made us think this place is unventured". That was it. We finally started connecting dots.

"So, the cobwebs are fake. Does that mean the algae are too?" Lewis went and touched the algae.

"Just as I thought... It's fake." "So, someone made a fake haunted house, someone sure used the reputation to keep people away! But for what?? We didn't find any details regarding Mr. Wiese." After I completed my sentence, Ben suddenly jumped up and gave a twirl. "Come with me comrades." He took us up to the second bedroom in front of the shelf. "Goodness gracious! How can someone drink this much wine!" Lewis exclaimed.

"That's not the point Lewis" I said, "this shelf is a fake ... And it's a door. Because it's not connected with the wall... but how can we open this ??" Ben said in one quick breath. We all started to think. Then, something struck me. "Guy's think, there is no clip or a latch, so this probably doesn't open like that. It hasn't got a sensor, so it is definitely not remote controlled."

"Then what is it?" all three of them said in a chorus. "It's simple," I answered. "The only props present here are the bottles. So, if we pull one of them ...the door will open. Now the question is which one. Look, in the 1800s there were a lot of popular wines, but not as popular as the "Barradas" from Madeira present in the bottom right corner."

Saying so I pulled it and the shelf instantly turned around like a door. Unfolded a solid brown coloured room behind, in which there was just a chair. "When did you have so much knowledge about wine?" asked Ben. "Must've paid attention in the Gk class Ben"I answered. This was probably the last conversation that we had.

I entered the room with others.... And instantly started to feel dizzy. "Arrree ... Youuu feeelllingggg Dizzzzzyyy?" Asked Harold and immediately collapsed, followed by Lewis. My eyes started to turn cloudy. "No ... This can't be "i thought. I don't remember anything after that.

When my eyes opened... I saw a man in a black overcoat standing in front of me with a grin in his face. His face seemed familiar. My friend was behind me... All tied up and their mouths taped. I was also tied up .... But my mouth was open.

"You surely must recognize me... Kiddo" started the man. Then it struck me. IT WAS THE SAME MAN ON THE NEWS. It was ...
"Yes, I am Joseph Wiese... The nephew of John Wiese.... All of this .... All was planned by me."

"But ... How and why did you do it? He was your unc-" I was cut off by his laughter. "You're such an innocent little kid. The old rack had kept all of his property to himself. I was waiting for him to pass away. But when my three attempts of poisoning him failed, I understood this geezer wouldn't die so easily. So, I kidnapped him. Gave away the hints myself, and obviously... acted as if I couldn't deal with his disappearance and cried, oh that innocent officer, you know that whack even comforted me! But anyways, he won't be found soon and I will slowly poison him to death anyways. As the sole surviving relative I'll get the inheritance in 7 years time. In the mean time I'll ship this fossil of an uncle off to an old age home in Russia. Already booked his ticket, and the case would also close officially soon. Gosh I'm so happy." All these words disgusted me. "You" I started "are a pig. A disgrace to your family. Even after all your uncle has been through ... you didn't even have a little mercy. And you are calling him names? He was the one to give you such a life after your parents passed away. You should kiss his feet." "Oh, shut up portable kid... You haven't seen the world. It's a very bad place. You don't find "kind" people anymore. The one who is sly, thrives. Others! Well get scraped off ... like my uncle will. Grow up! And you'll understand.
"That doesn't justify kidnapping your own blood. The one that brought you up. The one that gave you a roof. The one that ensured that you never felt the grief of losing your parents!"

Joseph seemed furious. I could see his forehead veins popping out of his pale skin. "You'll regret this kid... I'll have to poison you, it seems "I could hear muffled screams from behind. It was from my three musketeers. They would face the same fate as me. I couldn't believe how I just wasted 4 lives. I can never forgive myself. I could hear thudding sounds. "Oh, my crazy uncle is banging on the door of the room again!" Joseph blurted out turning towards a small trapdoor at the back wall of the room, but it seemed like it wasn't Mr Wiese who was banging as the sound came from the front door!

It was indeed Mr.Walter, our officer in charge, who banged open the front door and entered with armed officers. "Mr.Joseph Wiese, you are under arrest for kidnapping and allegedly poisoning your uncle. You have the right to remain silent."

Joseph was dumbstruck. He tried to act cool "officer you must be mistaken. I came to investigate and found these kids tied here. I was helping them." "Cut the crap" the officer said. We heard your so-called 'plan' through our recorder... you think we are that foolish?"

Recorder? How on earth was there a recorder? But then I realized... Why Harold was so quiet! Why was he 'suddenly' carrying a black slick backpack?

Seemed like he had already contacted the police through his uncle who was police himself and they advised him to take the recorder with him. Joseph made a big mistake underestimating us as kids and he took no preparation. And he had to pay for it.
Old Mr.Wiese was freed, and we were thanked specially by the government. The next day we were in the newspaper. It was a dream come true. Our courage helped us identify a criminal and save a man's life! It was wonderful. And ... It gave us experience which started off a whole lot of new things. This was indeed the beginning of something, our Investigator Team of Tinkletown!

Chapter 1: The Invitation

In the twilight's embrace, as the sun began its descent, casting long shadows across the quaint town, Ronald's phone buzzed with an unexpected invitation. It was from his close friend, Ethan, who had always possessed an adventurous spirit.

"Hey, Ethan," Ronald answered, his voice laced with curiosity.

"Ronald, it's me!" Ethan exclaimed, his voice crackling with excitement. "My parents are out of town tonight, and I'm having a sleepover. You in?"

A surge of delight coursed through Ronald's veins. Sleepovers with Ethan were always filled with laughter, mischief, and the thrill of forbidden adventures. "Of course, I'm in!" he replied enthusiastically.

"Awesome!" Ethan said. "Bring some snacks and drinks. I'll have the games and movies ready. "Ronald hung up the phone and couldn't contain his excitement. He had been looking forward to a sleepover with Ethan for weeks, and now it was finally happening. With a mischievous grin, he grabbed a bag and began to fill it with an assortment of pizzas, burgers, cold drinks, chips, and other treats. As he made his way to Ethan's house, the evening air was thick with anticipation. The moon hung high in the sky, casting an eerie glow upon the town. Ronald couldn't shake the feeling that something extraordinary was about to unfold. Upon arriving at Ethan's house, Ronald was greeted by the sound of loud music and the smell of freshly cooked food. Ethan opened the door with a wide smile and pulled Ronald inside.

"Welcome, my friend!" Ethan said, giving Ronald a high-five.

"The party's just getting started."

Chapter 2: The Sleepover

As darkness enveloped the neighborhood, Ronald and I settled into his cozy bedroom for a night of slumber and revelry. The air crackled with anticipation as we awaited the arrival of our gastronomic feast. Moments later, the doorbell rang, and Ronald dashed to answer it. A delivery boy stood on the doorstep, laden with an assortment of culinary delights. We eagerly carried the bounty into the room and spread it out on the bed .Pizza boxes, brimming with melted cheese and savory toppings, beckoned us. Burgers, juicy and succulent, tantalized our taste buds. Cold drinks, their condensation glistening, promised to quench our thirst. And crispy chips, golden brown and irresistible, completed our culinary symphony. With ravenous appetites, we devoured our feast.

The pizza slices disappeared with alarming speed, leaving only greasy remnants on our fingers. The burgers were demolished with equal enthusiasm, their savory juices dripping down our chins. As we indulged in our culinary extravaganza, the conversation flowed effortlessly. We shared stories of our childhoods, our hopes and dreams, and our secret fears. Laughter and camaraderie filled the room, creating an atmosphere of warmth and intimacy.

As the night wore on, our energy levels began to dwindle. We stretched out on the bed, our bellies full and our spirits content. The gentle glow of the bedside lamp cast a warm and inviting light, lulling us into a state of drowsiness. One by one, our eyelids grew heavy and our breathing became shallow. The sounds of the outside world faded into a distant hum, replaced by the rhythmic beating of our own hearts. And as the darkness enveloped us, we drifted into a realm of dreams, where the horrors that awaited us in the old graveyard were still unknown.

Chapter 3: The Games

As the sun began its descent, casting long shadows across Ronald's backyard, we found ourselves with nothing more to occupy our time. The PlayStation controller lay idle on the couch, and the pizza boxes were empty. "Hey," Ronald suggested, breaking the silence, "let's play some games.

"I nodded in agreement. "Sure, what do you have in mind?" Ronald grinned. "I've got a deck of cards in my room. How about some poker?"

We retrieved the cards and settled back on the couch. As we dealt the first hands, the atmosphere in the room transformed. The laughter and chatter of the earlier hours faded away, replaced by a tense focus. We played for hours, the stakes rising with each game. Ronald proved to be a formidable opponent, his sharp wit and keen eye for bluffing giving him a distinct advantage. I managed to win a few hands, but Ronald consistently came out on top.

As the night wore on, we switched to video games. Ronald's PlayStation 4 held a treasure trove of titles, and we couldn't resist diving into the virtual worlds they offered. We battled zombies in Call of Duty, raced cars in Forza Horizon, and competed in online matches of Fortnite. Time flew by as we immersed ourselves in the digital realms. The outside world seemed to fade away, replaced by the vibrant landscapes and adrenaline-pumping action on the screen. We shouted, laughed, and cursed as we navigated the challenges and celebrated our victories. Finally, as the clock ticked past midnight, we realized that we couldn't stay awake any longer. The games had exhausted us, both physically and mentally. With heavy eyelids, we stumbled to our feet and headed to Ronald's bedroom. As we lay down on the bed, I couldn't help but feel a sense of contentment. The night had been filled with laughter, excitement, and the unwavering bond of friendship. And as I drifted off to sleep, I knew that the memories of this sleepover would stay with me for a lifetime.

Chapter 4: The Suggestion

As the night wore on, the excitement of the evening began to wane. We had exhausted all our gaming options and were starting to feel restless.

"What should we do now?" Ronald asked, boredom etched across his face. We sat in silence for a moment, contemplating our options. Suddenly, Ronald's eyes lit up. "Hey, I have an idea," he exclaimed. "Let's check out the old cemetery here!" I blinked in surprise. "The cemetery? At this hour?"

"Yeah, why not?" Ronald shrugged. "It's not like anyone's there. "A shiver ran down my spine at the thought of venturing into a graveyard in the dead of night. But I couldn't deny the allure of the unknown.

"Okay," I said hesitantly. "But let's be quick about it." Ronald grinned. "Don't worry, we'll be back before you know it. "With that, we grabbed our jackets and headed out into the cool night air. The cemetery was just a short walk from Ronald's house, but the darkness seemed to close in around us as we approached. As we reached the wrought-iron gates, a gust of wind slammed them shut behind us, sending a chill through our bodies. We stood there for a moment, listening to the eerie silence.

"Are you sure about this?" I whispered. "Don't be a baby," Ronald scoffed. "It's just a graveyard. "He pushed open the gates and we stepped inside. The moonlight cast an ethereal glow on the tombstones, creating an otherworldly atmosphere. We wandered through the rows of graves, reading the names and dates etched into the stone. Some of the graves were ancient, their inscriptions faded with time. Others were more recent, with fresh flowers adorning them. As we walked, I couldn't shake the feeling that we were being watched. I glanced over my shoulder every few steps, expecting to see something lurking in the shadows.

Suddenly, Ronald stopped in his tracks. "Look," he said, pointing to a particularly large and elaborate tombstone.

We approached the grave and read the inscription: "Here lies William Blackwood, the notorious grave robber. May his soul find peace." A chill ran down my spine. I had heard stories about William Blackwood, a man who had been hanged for robbing graves. It was said that his ghost still haunted the cemetery, searching for his lost treasures. "Let's get out of here," I said, my voice trembling. But Ronald was unfazed. "Don't be silly," he said. "It's just a story. "He reached out and touched the tombstone. As his fingers brushed against the cold stone, a faint glow emanated from the grave. We both gasped in surprise and jumped back.

"What was that?" I asked.

Ronald shook his head. "I don't know," he said. "But I think we should go."And with that, we turned and ran out of the cemetery, the gates swinging open as if by magic.

Chapter 5: The Graveyard

As darkness enveloped the town, Ronald and I embarked on our eerie adventure to the old cemetery. The air grew heavy with anticipation as we approached the wrought-iron gates, their creaking hinges a sinister welcome. We stepped into the hallowed ground, our footsteps echoing through the silent tombstones. The moon cast an ethereal glow upon the graves, casting long, ominous shadows that danced and twisted in the dim light.

We wandered aimlessly, our eyes scanning the weathered inscriptions. Names and dates long forgotten stared back at us, a chilling reminder of the passage of time. As we ventured deeper into the cemetery, the air grew colder, and a sense of unease crept over me. Suddenly, a noise broke the silence. A faint scratching sound seemed to come from behind one of the tombstones. We froze, our hearts pounding in our chests. Slowly, we approached the source of the noise. As we peered around the tombstone, we gasped in horror. There, lying on the ground, was a human skull. Its empty eye sockets stared up at us, filled with an eerie emptiness. We stumbled backward, our minds reeling from the gruesome discovery. Fear propelled us forward, and we ran as fast as our legs could carry us. The cemetery seemed to close in around us, the tombstones like silent sentinels bearing witness to our terror.

Finally, we reached the gates and burst through, panting and breathless.

Chapter 6: The Terrifying Encounter

As we fled through the overgrown cemetery, the darkness enveloped us like a suffocating blanket. Our breaths came in ragged gasps as we stumbled over uneven ground, desperate to escape the horrors we had witnessed. Suddenly, a piercing scream echoed through the night, sending shivers down our spines. We froze in our tracks, our eyes darting around in search of the source. A cold breeze swept through the trees, carrying with it a faint whisper that seemed to call our names. Fear gnawed at our minds as we cautiously approached the direction of the scream. As we rounded a towering tombstone, we came face to face with a sight that chilled us to the bone. There, in the flickering moonlight, stood a shadowy figure. Its form was tall and emaciated, its eyes glowing with an otherworldly intensity. Its long, bony fingers reached out towards us, as if it sought to drag us into the depths of darkness. We let out a collective gasp and stumbled backward, tripping over a fallen branch. As we lay on the ground, helpless and terrified, the figure advanced slowly. Its footsteps echoed through the silent graveyard, each step sending a wave of dread through our bodies.

"Run!" Ethan whispered hoarsely. With renewed desperation, we scrambled to our feet and fled once more. But the figure pursued us relentlessly, its movements swift and silent. We could hear its heavy breathing behind us, growing louder with each passing moment. As we reached the edge of the cemetery, we realized that the gate was locked. Panic surged through us as we frantically searched for a way out. But there was no escape. The figure had us cornered.

Chapter 7: The Haunted History

As we stumbled away from the gruesome skull, we couldn't shake the feeling that we had stumbled upon something truly sinister. The cemetery seemed to close in around us, its ancient stones whispering secrets we couldn't decipher. Determined to unravel the mystery, we approached an elderly woman sitting on a bench nearby. Her eyes held a distant look, as if she had witnessed countless horrors within these hallowed grounds. "Excuse me, ma'am," Ronald began, his voice trembling. "Do you know anything about the skull we just found?" The woman sighed and looked at us with pity.

"Ah, yes, the skull of poor old Samuel. He was a caretaker here many years ago, a kind and gentle soul. But one fateful night, he was brutally murdered by a group of vandals. "Her voice dropped to a whisper. "They say his ghost still haunts the cemetery, seeking revenge on those who wronged him." A shiver ran down our spines. The legend of Samuel's ghost had been passed down for generations, but we had never given it much credence. Now, with the gruesome discovery of his skull, it all seemed so real. "Is there anything we can do to help?" I asked, my voice barely above a murmur.

The woman shook her head sadly. "There is no rest for Samuel until his killer is brought to justice. But the vandals were never caught, and their identities remain a mystery." As we left the cemetery that night, the shadows seemed to dance and the wind whispered secrets we couldn't understand. The haunted history of Samuel's ghost lingered in our minds, casting a dark shadow over our hearts. In that situation it didn't occur to us that it is very strange that we should meet an old lady at that hour of night who would calmly answer our questions.

Chapter 8: The Escape from the Graveyard

Our hearts pounded in our chests as we stumbled through the darkness, desperate to escape the clutches of the haunted graveyard. The eerie silence was broken only by the sound of our own ragged breaths. As we ran, the tombstones seemed to blur into grotesque shapes, their shadows dancing and twisting around us. Fear propelled us forward, our legs burning with exhaustion. Suddenly, a cold hand brushed against Ronald's shoulder. He screamed and stumbled, nearly falling. I reached out to grab him, but his fingers slipped through the darkness. "Ronald!" I cried out. But there was no answer. Panic surged through me as I realized Ronald was gone. I frantically searched the surrounding area, but my friend had vanished into thin air. With a heavy heart, I knew I had to continue without Ronald. I ran with renewed determination, my eyes scanning every shadow for a sign of danger. As I approached the bent away from the Graveyard lane, a faint glow appeared in the distance. It was the light of the streetlamps, a beacon of safety that seemed a lifetime away. Summoning my last ounce of strength, I surged forward and burst through the gates. I collapsed on the pavement, gasping for air. As I lay there, my body trembling with exhaustion and fear, I couldn't shake the feeling that something sinister still lurked within the shadows of the graveyard. But for now, I was safe. I had escaped the Gruesome Graveyard, but the horrors I had witnessed would forever haunt my nightmares. What started as an adventure ended in a macabre accident and I would never know what happened to Ronald. I must have slept off as when I woke up, I saw a bunch of people staring down at me questioningly. Looking at a policeman in the group I jumped up and related my piece requesting him to look for Ronald. As the search progressed a constable looked at me and asked me to describe the old lady. On hearing what little I could tell he nodded and said "looks Martha, Samuel's wife, but she too died a year back out of heartbreak!" Before I could process the information, we were alerted by a scream from the search party, and as I approached the area, they now stood encircling, the limp form of Ronald came into view! He was cold dead, his face still contorted in fear and eyes popped out as if he had seen a ghost!

www.ingramcontent.com/pod-product-compliance
Lightning Source LLC
LaVergne TN
LVHW061627070526
838199LV00070B/6605